Dear Parents:

Congratulations! Your child is taking the first steps on an exciting journey. The destination? Independent reading!

STEP INTO READING® will help your child get there. The program offers five steps to reading success. Each step includes fun stories and colorful art or photographs. In addition to original fiction and books with favorite characters, there are Step into Reading Non-Fiction Readers, Phonics Readers and Boxed Sets, Sticker Readers, and Comic Readers—a complete literacy program with something to interest every child.

Learning to Read, Step by Step!

Ready to Read   Preschool–Kindergarten
• big type and easy words • rhyme and rhythm • picture clues
For children who know the alphabet and are eager to begin reading.

Reading with Help   Preschool–Grade 1
• basic vocabulary • short sentences • simple stories
For children who recognize familiar words and sound out new words with help.

Reading on Your Own   Grades 1–3
• engaging characters • easy-to-follow plots • popular topics
For children who are ready to read on their own.

Reading Paragraphs   Grades 2–3
• challenging vocabulary • short paragraphs • exciting stories
For newly independent readers who read simple sentences with confidence.

Ready for Chapters   Grades 2–4
• chapters • longer paragraphs • full-color art
For children who want to take the plunge into chapter books but still like colorful pictures.

STEP INTO READING® is designed to give every child a successful reading experience. The grade levels are only guides; children will progress through the steps at their own speed, developing confidence in their reading. The F&P Text Level on the back cover serves as another tool to help you choose the right book for your child.

Remember, a lifetime love of reading starts with a single step!

For Drummer

Text copyright © 2021 by Suzanne Lang
Cover art and interior illustrations copyright © 2021 by Max Lang

All rights reserved. Published in the United States by Random House Children's Books,
a division of Penguin Random House LLC, New York.

Step into Reading, Random House, and the Random House colophon are registered trademarks
of Penguin Random House LLC.

GRUMPY MONKEY is a registered trademark of Pick & Flick Pictures, Inc.

Visit us on the Web!
StepIntoReading.com
rhcbooks.com

Educators and librarians, for a variety of teaching tools, visit us at RHTeachersLibrarians.com

Library of Congress Cataloging-in-Publication Data is available upon request.
ISBN 978-0-593-42832-0 (trade) — ISBN 978-0-593-42833-7 (lib. bdg.) —
ISBN 978-0-593-42863-4 (ebook)

Printed in the United States of America
10 9 8 7 6 5 4 3 2 1

This book has been officially leveled by using
the F&P Text Level Gradient™ Leveling System.

STEP INTO READING®

STEP 2

READING WITH HELP

GRUMPY MONKEY
Get Your Grumps Out

by Suzanne Lang
illustrated by Max Lang

Random House 🏠 New York

Jim Panzee

was stomping around.

"Why are you stomping, Jim?" asked Norman.

"I need to get
all my grumps out,"
said Jim.
"Tomorrow is a New Year,
and I will be a new me."

Norman scratched
his head.

Jim called his friends.
"Hey, everybody.
Come help me get
my grumps out."

First, Tortoise ate
the very last banana.
"Does that make
you grumpy?"
asked Oxpecker.
"Yes!" said Jim.

Then Tortoise
threw the peel
on the ground.
"Does that make
you grumpy?"
asked Oxpecker.

"Yes!" said Jim.

Jim stomped and stomped.

But he still had
some grumps left.
"Someone else try."

Water Buffalo told Jim
to clean up his tree.

Jim stomped and cleaned.

Rhino made

a great big rhino fart.

Jim stomped and yelled.
But he still had
a few grumps left.

Norman came over
holding a branch.
"I broke your branch.
I am sorry,"
said Norman.
"I did not mean
to do it."

Now Jim was extra
super-duper grumpy!
Jim stomped and yelled
and yelled and stomped.

At last
he could not yell
or stomp anymore.
Then Jim smiled.
"It worked!" he said.

Jim felt happy.
"Thank you, everybody.
I got all my
grumps out," he said.

Happy New Jim had a great New Year's Eve with his friends.

They helped him
pick a new branch.
It was just above
his old one.

They had
a yummy dinner.
They played games.

And then they
counted down
to midnight.

The next day,
Oxpecker woke Jim up
early with her singing.
"Happy New Year!"

Jim did not like
waking up early.
He felt grumpy.

Jim stomped and stomped.

Oxpecker flew

out of the way.

"What about
the new you?"
said Oxpecker.

"I forgot," said Jim.

He felt bad.

"I was not the new me

for very long,"

said Jim.

Norman came down
from his tree.
"That is okay," he said.
"It is better to be
the real you."

That made Jim feel good.
"Grumpy New Year,
Norman," said Jim.
"Grumpy New Year, Jim,"
said Norman.